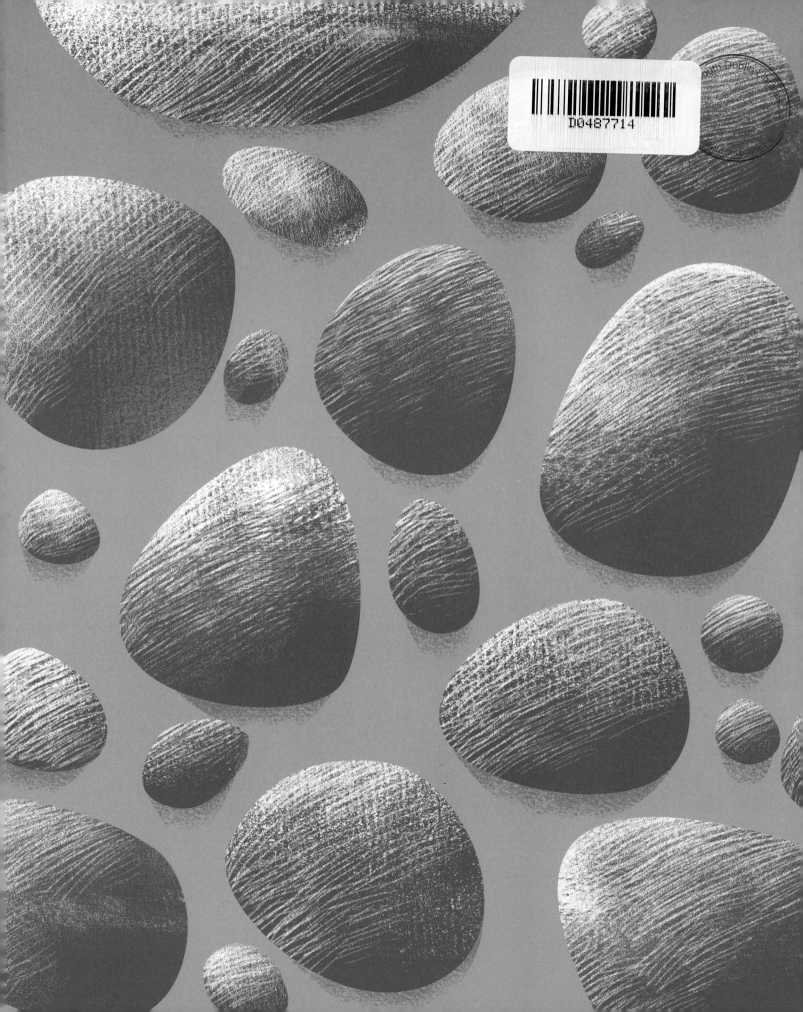

WILLOW
THE ARMADILLO

words by Marilou Reeder
pictures by Dave Mottram

Abrams Books for Young Readers • New York

LIBRARY

Ever since she was a tiny armadillo,
Willow loved picture books.

She borrowed as many from the library as her arms could carry.

"One day I'll be in a picture book of my own,"
she'd whisper, poring over the pages.

Being in the background wasn't an option—no.
She wanted to be the one to save the day,
the character everyone looked up to.
Willow wanted to be the hero.

Her parents tried to tell her it was a long shot.
"You have a tough shell, sweetie,
but heroes are strong and brave!"
"A hero? You have quite the imagination."

Still, Willow's dream persisted. She signed up to take classes at Picture Book Academy under the legendary Madame Tigress.

The other students doubted her,
but that didn't stop Willow.

She studied hard, learned to identify animals in distress,

"Excellent!"

and practiced lifting heavy objects.

"That's it!"

Each night, Willow repeated what Madame Tigress told her:
"Show them your heroic heart,
and you will surely get the part."

PICTURE BOOK HERO TRYOUTS

JUDGE

JIMMY'S MONSTER

After graduation,
Willow was ready.

She put on her bravest
face and tried out to be
a bedtime hero.

"Not what we're looking for. Next!"

Willow knew she needed to keep trying.
At her next audition, she flexed her muscles and went for it.

"Um, I don't think so.
Next!"

It crossed her mind that maybe she needed to change her image.
She became Arma Dynamo,

but it didn't help.

"Not the right fit, sorry."   **"Negative."**

Willow tried to stay positive,
but with each rejection,

her dream seemed more and more distant.

One day, she saw a sign.

YOU COULD BE
THE
NEXT
PICTURE
BOOK
HERO!

CASTING CALL!

This would be her big break!

"Sorry, but we've already found someone for the job."

Willow felt so low, she curled into a ball and
stayed that way for hours.
Then she rolled to the library.

Being surrounded by books usually made her feel better.
But all she could see were her classmates
on their covers.

Just then, the library went dark.

CRASH!

HELP!

MOMMY!

It was chaos!
Willow sprang into action.

WAAAAA!

I CAN'T
SEE!

Willow took the tiny book light she carried in her pocket and held it up. "Walk carefully toward me," she called.

She asked everyone to sit down.
She dried tears.
And she read them her favorite stories
until the lights came on.

"Willow, you saved the day!" said Ms. Dotty, the librarian.
Everyone cheered!

The next day, Willow visited the library
and found a surprise waiting for her.

They'd made her a book of her own.
"I love it! Thank you!" she said.

She looked at all the smiling faces,
and her heart felt big.

Someday she might go to another audition. But for now?
Nothing could top being a hero in real life.
"Who wants to read a story?"

For Jack, who regularly saves the day
—M.R.

For Dad
—D.M.

The art in this book was created with pencil and digital texture brushes in Photoshop.

Cataloging-in-Publication Data has been applied for and may be obtained from the Library of Congress.

ISBN 978-1-4197-4105-0

Published in 2020 by Abrams Books for Young Readers, an imprint of ABRAMS.

Printed and bound in China
10 9 8 7 6 5 4 3 2 1

Abrams Books for Young Readers are available at special discounts when purchased in quantity for premiums and promotions as well as fundraising or educational use. Special editions can also be created to specification. For details, contact specialsales@abramsbooks.com or the address below.

ABRAMS The Art of Books
195 Broadway, New York, NY 10007
abramsbooks.com